MW00964398

How the Squirrel got his stripes

Illustrations: Alex Stewart
Text: Sam Perera

Popsicle Books

Published by
Popsicle Books, 2015
an imprint of the Perera Hussein Publishing House
www.pererahussein.com

ISBN: 978-955-0041-08-4

How the Squirrel got his Stripes is a folk tale inspired by *the Ramayana*,
re-told by Sam Perera to Alex Stewart.

First Edition

Printed and bound by Samayawardhana Printers (pvt)Ltd.

To offset the environmental pollution caused by printing books,
the Perera Hussein Publishing House grows trees in Puttalam,
Sri Lanka's semi-arid zone.

This book
belongs to:

Rama, a dutiful prince, and rightful heir to the throne of Ayodhya, was expelled from his father's kingdom and sent to the forest for a number of years by his aunt Kaikeyi, who wanted kingship for her son.

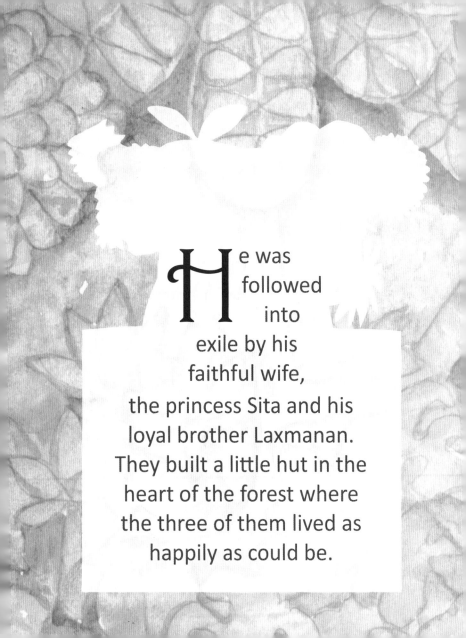

He was followed into exile by his faithful wife, the princess Sita and his loyal brother Laxmanan. They built a little hut in the heart of the forest where the three of them lived as happily as could be.

One day, Rama went hunting with Laxmanan. Drawing a magic circle around their hut, he told Sita that as long as she stayed inside the circle she would be safe.

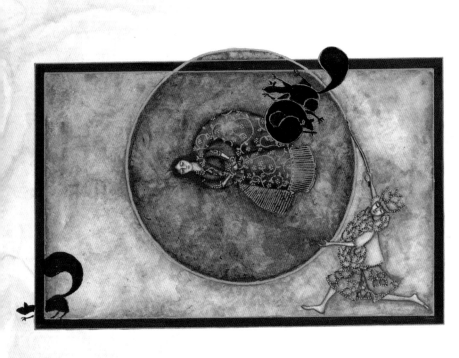

But while Rama was away hunting, Ravana the king of Lanka tricked Sita out of the magic circle. Jatayu the old vulture tried to rescue her.

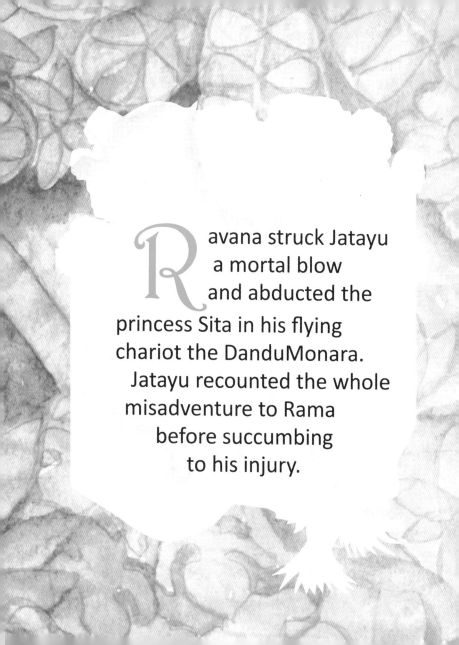

Ravana struck Jatayu a mortal blow and abducted the princess Sita in his flying chariot the DanduMonara. Jatayu recounted the whole misadventure to Rama before succumbing to his injury.

The DanduMonara sped through the air, carrying Ravana and the princess Sita far, far away to the City of Lanka.

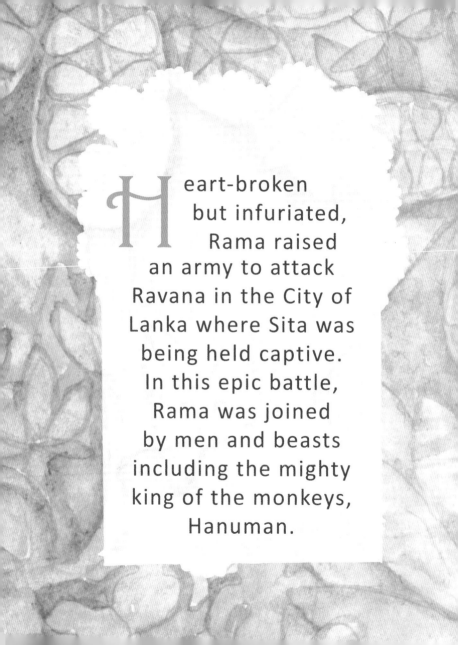

Heart-broken but infuriated, Rama raised an army to attack Ravana in the City of Lanka where Sita was being held captive. In this epic battle, Rama was joined by men and beasts including the mighty king of the monkeys, Hanuman.

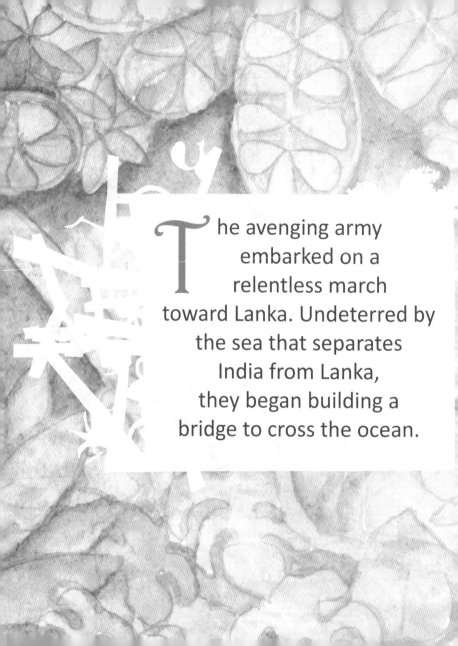

The avenging army embarked on a relentless march toward Lanka. Undeterred by the sea that separates India from Lanka, they began building a bridge to cross the ocean.

Men and animals worked hand-in-hand to complete the bridge as fast as possible. Everyone did their part. They were joined by beautiful, jet black squirrels who were too small to carry stones or do heavy work.

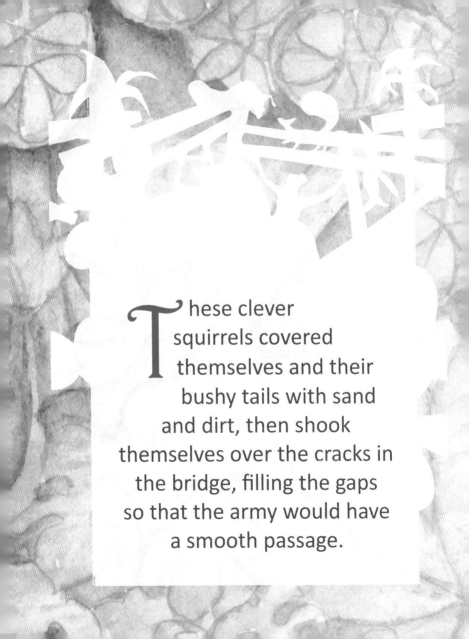

These clever squirrels covered themselves and their bushy tails with sand and dirt, then shook themselves over the cracks in the bridge, filling the gaps so that the army would have a smooth passage.

When the bridge was complete, Rama who was as good as he was great, thanked everyone individually. Rama picked up the squirrel and while thanking it, stroked its dusty back with his sweaty fingers.

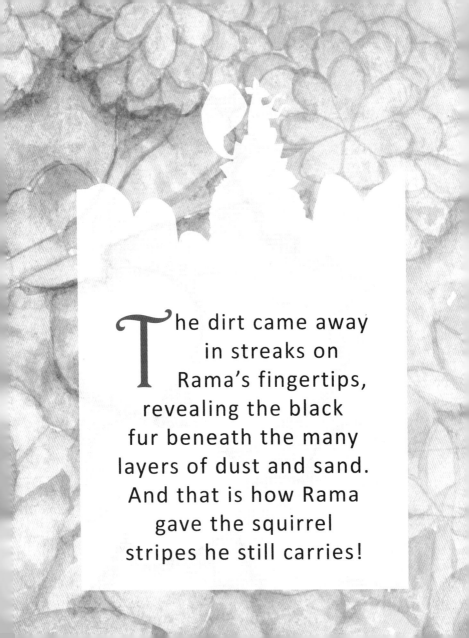

The dirt came away in streaks on Rama's fingertips, revealing the black fur beneath the many layers of dust and sand. And that is how Rama gave the squirrel stripes he still carries!

This book will soon be available in
Sinhala and Tamil from Popsicle Books.

Popsicle Books is an imprint of the
Perera-Hussein Publishing House,
dedicated to publishing high quality
children's books which have a
positive educative or socio-cultural impact.

www.pererahussein.com
info@pererahussein.com